ISBN 978-1-312-32096-3

Reflections

Christina Page

Depression

Unhappiness
November or December 2010

Sitting in the room all alone – wondering what is going on?
Moving on is so hard, what is there to do, everything seems gone.

How do you know nothing is there? When should you just end it all?
No trust, no love, no happiness, should you even bother with one las call?

All you want is to be happy; all you want is the pain to go away.
The one person who seems to make things better is also the one person who never can stay.

You just want to run and hide, to leave everything behind.
You wish to go back to the way things were, when people were actually kind.

You want away, you want to leave, and you want to get out of this place.
It's not possible, you have to go to school, you try to move on and put on a happy face.

You want to run your own life; you want to cause your own pain.
People tell you things will get better, but you don't see how anything is to gain.

You look in the mirror and what or who do you see?
Unhappiness, disappointment, someone you wish you didn't have to be.

People tell you you're pretty, people tell you that you make them proud.
You can't believe them, you don't feel special, and you feel like just another face in the crowd.

Disappointment rounds every corner, at home it's like walking on glass.
Everything changes, everything's different, in life all that matters is wanting to pass.

People bother you; you pull away from your friends.
You look at your future, you get scared, and you can't wait until it all ends.

What's the point, does anything matter, and are most things even of any value to keep?
Depression haunts, pain creeps in, you only know one escape, and you want only to sleep.

The thoughts you think, me things you want to do scare even yourself.
You sit in a room, you look around, and you see the scissors on the shelf.

You're at that point, you don't know what to do, and the pain is deep inside your core.
You're lost in unhappiness; you walk by and pull the knife from your drawer.

You want to control the pain, but you're too scared to make your razor cut your thumb or wrist in the shower.
You try to be tough, you try to be strong, but you're actually weak and you just want to cower.

What is there to do with your pain and your life? How can you be in control?
Your life is your story, but it feels like you're not even in the leading role.

You scream "will anyone listen, will anyone help me, and please someone help me."
What to do, where to go, you just want to be set free.

"Set me free, please let me go", you desperately cry.
People tell you "God will set you free", but you can't tell it right now, why?

Everything goes wrong, everything is falling apart, it seems like your whole life is falling down the drain.
You stand outside, but unlike most people you actually like to be out in the rain.

Some friends try really hard, but you just get aggravated because you don't want to smile.
As some try, others don't, and the ones who don't are the ones who end up making you happy all the while.

What to do, where to go, how will things ever be back to normal?
Your whole life things were perfect, and until now things were formal.

The days go by slow, when will they end? But thankfully the weeks go by fast.
Although time continues to pass, all you want is things to be good, like they were in the past.

What to do, why to care, why won't it all just stop?
Your mind is spinning, your face is burning, it feels like your head is about to pop.

People wonder and people stop to stare as the tears fall down your cheek.
Unlike what you used to do, you now willingly agree that you are mentally and emotionally weak.

Others seem to know what the outcome of your actions will be, but you don't because of your lack of savviness.
You feel trapped, you want to get out, and you're surrounded by unhappiness, unhappiness, unhappiness.

The Feeling of…
September 11, 2011

I'm tired of people knowing "how I feel".
I'm tired of everything; I want something that is real.

I always feel sick, I never want to eat.
I hate this spot light, I want out of this heat.

These feelings I have, I don't want to think.
I wish I could live, be and not freak.

One day I'm fine, the next day I'm not.
Something will trigger it and my face will go hot.

I'm always tired but I don't want to sleep.
I honestly don't feel like I'm worthy to keep.

What's the point, what does it matter?
I want it to end, please stop the batter.

How can they know what your feelings are?
When inside of you they can't see that far.

Why bother, why should I try?
When no matter what I'll always cry.

I give up, no one really cares.
All I can feel are these rips and tears.

I have to be around people, yet I like it by myself.
I feel that if love is money then I have no wealth.

I don't know what to do or where to go.
I feel as if I have nothing to show.

Why is this going on, my heart is breaking?
I feel it every day, my body aching.

Why does this happen, must it go on?
Why can't everything be new just like the dawn?

I feel guilty; I convince myself everything is my fault.
People tell me not to think, but I can't take everything as a grain of salt.

It blocks out everything, but the pain gets to me.
My heart is breaking; I just want to be set free.

I don't know what to do; I'm in over my head.
The only place I'm okay is in my bed.

My bed is my safe zone; it's where I can cry.
There no one can hurt me, and I don't have to try.

It feels weird not being on the phone.
I don't like it, being on my own.

People see me, but they don't understand.
They try to help, but they don't get what is at hand.

Last year's feelings come back so quickly.
No matter what I do I end up feeling sickly.

I want it to end, just to all go away.
It's only been a week, and already I pull astray.

I feel the guilt, I feel the pain.
I believe there's nothing left to gain.

The stress of everything throws me into a fit.
I just can't wait to get the hang of it.

I shouldn't feel alone, I'm in a crowded place.
But no one can see me, I'm just another face.

Every day I see something that triggers a thought.
Reminds me of the outcome; of the fight I fought.

The words I hear, I know they're right.
But in order to believe them I'd have to fight.

The feelings I feel every day are mixed.
I just wish all these problems will soon be fixed.

I want it to end, to all go away.
I don't want to feel like this, not for another day.

Sometimes I feel that everything is good.
But most of the time I feel things aren't going the way they should.

I'm longing and waiting for that day.
When "I'm over it" is something I can honestly say.

Convincing
September 14, 2011

The mind is a powerful thing.
Sometimes it makes me feel like I'm at a circus in the middle of the ring.

My mind convinces me that I'm not worth it.
It tells me that I'll never find a group I'll fit.

Convincing myself that the world wouldn't miss me.
Even though people say they would, I just can't see it.

I feel the world would e a better place.
If there was just one less face.

I have a good day and actually have some fun.
Then my mind tells me the pain isn't quite done.

I know I will feel better after writing.
But my thoughts and the words are fighting.

I finally started to actually want a meal.
But once again I'm scared to eat because of how my stomach will feel.

My mind convinces me that everything is wrong.
And no matter how hard I try, I can't stay strong.

I want to be around people, have fun, and go out.
But every time I do my mind is filled with doubt.

I wish I could draw, I feel it would be better self-expression.
I think it would help me more when hit by depression.

I feel that I should and need to pray.
But I'm at a loss of words, and want nothing to say.

Worthless
November 24, 2013

I fight these feelings, but to no avail.
My self-confidence and self worth are ever so frail.

I base my worth on how guys look at me, and if I'm worth sleeping with.
But if you ask me, I plead the fifth.

Unwanted I sit alone.
With the weight of the world I feel left on my own.

The only thing in the world that needs me is my dog.
The rest of the world seems hazy in a fog.

The words I long for, they never come.
All I here is my own heart beating like a drum.

Alone and upset most of my days are mirthless.
Unwanted, all the time I feel worthless.

Curve Ball

November 25, 2013

Confession, doubt, frustration, all overwhelming in feeling.
My mind races, the thoughts flood in, the outcomes unappealing.

Life had been drama free, and then you threw that curve ball.
I hate it; I want to be mad; no matter what happens I'm going to fall.

On one end I'm getting what I was longing for.
On another I'm faced with a situation I SHOULDN'T want anymore.

The longing, the wanting, it's all outweighed by the lack of trust.
It's the number one feeling, and rebuild it I must.

Lost in my own head, I've hit an emotional wall.
Everything was okay, until you threw this curve ball.

Alone
January 16, 2014

Confusion runs over me, I'm totally thrown.
In a room full of people, and I'm 100% alone.

No emotion, little laughter. I feel as cold as stone.
No matter how good my day has been I am always alone.

Waiting on something or someone I constantly check my phone.
It rarely has anything to tell; even it makes me feel alone.

Good days, bad days no matter my mood I'm still on my own.
Scared, unwanted, unloved, and totally alone.

Fear

January 16, 2014

On the outside looking in, I'm drowning in fear.
Nowhere to go, nowhere to fit in; not there nor here.

Lost and alone, forever confused.
When asked how I'm doing, to give an answer I refused.

I don't know who I am or where I belong.
I want me back; I used to be so strong.

People say I need God, but I can't even find myself.
I know that's not how it works, but my decisions have greatly
wounded my spiritual health.

The confusion and the want leave a pain that is searing.
I do hope this is not forever, my constant fearing.

Confusion
January 22, 2014

Confusion courses rapidly through my veins.
Accessing the situation, no matter the outcome, for someone it will be filled with pain.

I don't know what to do or why I feel this way.
These words, these thoughts I want so badly, but I just cannot say.

What do I want, are these feelings real?
My venerability and my fear, did they cause what I feel?

Does it even matter what I want?
Probably not, I guess I'll just go back to putting on a front.

I can swallow these feelings, just as long as I don't lose my friend.
That relationship I just can't let end.

The confusion I feel still courses through my veins.
Unfortunately I feel this is going to end in <u>my</u> pain.

Trust and Love
January 28, 2014

Trust is a gift, but one you must earn.
Trust is something to respect, not a bridge you should burn.

You have had my trust since the day we met.
Sure there were rough spots, but nothing that caused my trust to be off set.

My trust never wavered, but it leads to another feeling, too.
My trust leads to more, and soon I know that I love you.

With trust and love, I waited for something that would never be.
Hoping that one day you'll want to be with me.

That day finally came, and my decision was made.
I waited to tell you, and once I did you say your feelings did fade.

Trust and love, although we are over, only one went away.
My trust is gone, but I still love you today.

I don't know how long it will take, but eventually my love will go too.
I hope you are happy, on your own with just YOU!

I write these words to you, they are what I want to say.
But being the bigger person means I will keep quiet and turn away.

Decisions

June 23, 2014

Confusion runs through my blood.
My mind races; my thoughts flood.

A decision I made I now regret.
My undesirable feelings are my biggest threat.

Eventually these feelings will go away.
Can the feelings be lost, but the person stay?

The decision I made was not very smart.
I've gotten so good at bad decisions it's almost an art.

Eventually I will learn the right thing to do.
I think I need a new point of view.

One day I will learn, but today's not that day.
For now I will go, I have nothing left to say.

Happiness

When Tragedy Hits
Be Still and Know He is God
November 8, 2011

All my life I've heard stories of trauma and tragedy bringing people together, and I'd always hope I'd never have to go through it.
It always scared me that one little phone call could take everything, and throw it into a fit.

TV episodes would show tragedy and death, and every time I would fear.
Traumatic news, death, catastrophe, a phone call, anything telling me this type of news I never wanted to hear.

High school came around, we all learned to drive, I got a few phone calls of friends in wrecks, none of which were too severe.
Even though in all the wrecks all of my friends were okay, that news was something I didn't want to hear.

After that things were good, until the fourth of November.
On that day, while driving to band retreat, Kim and I received news that we will always remember.

My coworker Joe sent me a text "Are you okay?", but before all could be cleared up a call from another coworker James came in.
"Are you okay? Are you on the Ag bus?" "No, why?" "There's been a wreck." my head began to spin.

Kim and I started to make phone calls – at least four or five to each number known.
No one answered, other people didn't know, no updates were being shown.

I called Heather to let her know about the accident, and to tell her what I knew.
I told her I would call her if I found anything out, she said that she would too.

Allison, Anna, Marissa, and Naomi: these are the girls in class I sit next to.
Dr. C, Prof. M, Mrs. M, and Dr. N: some of the many people who think of us students in everything they do.

Anabel, Anna, Haley, Jason, Kathleen, Kendra, Mandy, and Tiffany: people I may not have known.
Classmates, professors, faces I recognized but didn't know, they all ran through my head, I had no information, my face turned white and I turned cold as stone.

A fire marshal who was on the scene gave us information we all wanted though our hearts it would greatly bother.
All but one were taken to the hospital, that one, Dear Anabel, went to be with our Heavenly Father.

I didn't have the privilege of knowing Anabel, but still my heart broke.
Her family, her friends, I wanted to help, but I could only stand frozen as the fire marshal spoke.

What do I do, how do I help, these people are my family here at school.
Feeling guilty and helpless, things my mind told me were cruel.

I put it behind me, I didn't matter, the ones who were hurt, they needed me.
Leaving retreat going back to campus, that's where I was supposed to be.

I couldn't see them, my emotions and fear of hospitals took control.
I can't listen to fear, I can't let it take over, no matter what I have to play my role.

At least a phone call or conversation through Skype, in some way I will contact my friends.
They need me, they need us, they will continue to need our department until all this turmoil ends.

We can't feel guilty, nothing could have been done, all we can do is pray and stick together in this time of need.
If one person stays strong, then a few more, eventually we'll all be strong after we follow the lead.

This is no one's fault, it couldn't have been helped, and there was no way of knowing what would lie ahead.
We have to be strong, for each other, though in times like this any tears will be shed.

Only God can get us through this, He will give us the power to comfort others.
We will get through this, we will prevail, we are one big family, sisters and brothers.

It's not every day something like this happens, but when tragedy hits, BE STILL AND KNOW THAT HE IS GOD!

No Need For Hate, Only For Love
April 28, 2011

Your life may not be great, but there is no reason for hate; for soon enough there will be a date. A date in which you will see, there is more that you can be; for God gave his Son for you to be free. To be free from all that hold you down, He wants to rid you of your frown; He wants you home in His town. His town above the world so high, far beyond any star in the sky; where you will always be able to fly. To fly from fear, hatred, and sadness; away from the badness, and into the gladness. Into gladness that only comes from above, that covers all of you like a glove; that can actually be seen as love. As love that can only come from The One, The Truth, The Heavenly Father, God.

Freedom

June 22, 2014

I'm going to try this again: writing for me.
Writing for me now that m brain is free.

Free from this drama, this mess I was in.
My brain was jumbled, in a constant spin.

But now I'm free, my thoughts all make sense.
All the pain and confusion is in past tense.

Freedom is wonderful, a feeling I quite enjoy.
These new thoughts and ideas I intend to employee.

Feeling

June 23, 2014

This feeling is one I don't know.
This smile is one I forgot to show.

Happiness is a feeling I have missed.
Sorrow and regret: goodbye I have kissed.

It is nice to be able to smile for real.
It took longer than I thought, but now I can heal.

This feeling, thought strange, is one I will keep.
One hurdle down, to the next I will leap.

Strength
June 23, 2014

For three years I thought I could do it on my own.
With my pen and my paper I could fix it alone.

My problems were mine, I didn't need any assistance.
Thought I thought I was getting healthy, I was only improving
my resistance.

Finally one day I hit a hard wall.
I wanted to kill myself, but decided to call.

I called my mom and told her my feeling.
She took me to a doctor to work on my dealing.

A week in the hospital and counseling thereafter.
Medication, thinking, and talking – these helped lead to now:
my happiness and laughter.

I'm not in the clear, please don't get me wrong.
But I'm working, I'm trying, I'm growing, and I'm strong.

Rhyme

June 24, 2014

I believe poems need to rhyme.
It helps the flow and helps the time.

Not all great poems sound the same.
But rhyme it must to bare my name.

Some of my best rhymes come as I lay in bed.
I must hurry to write them before they're lost in my head.

Once I start writing there isn't a rhyme I will miss.
What rhymes with that: hat and cat; what rhymes with this: hiss and kiss.

Poems don't have to rhyme, but I think they should.
They'd be more fun to read, and maybe more people would.

Yesterday
June 24, 2014

Yesterday sucked, but that won't stop me.
Today will be fine, for I am still free.

Free from the things that once held me down.
Today I will smile, though yesterday I wore a frown.

Today I will try to make the best.
Focus on what I can control and forget all the rest.

Yesterday is history, it's in the past.
Today I'll think of good things, because that's what needs to last.

Starting Over
June 24, 2014

Sometimes I wish I could start again.
To completely forget where I've been.

I want to start over, to start new.
It's an opportunity experienced by very few.

I'll clear my mind, I'll do my best.
I'll make my now better than the rest.

Rag Tyme

Written for RagTyme

As a part of Delta Tres Comics

Whisper
June 20, 2014

I hear the whisper of the wind.
Like a long lost friend.
Will it be there until the end?
I hear the whisper, where's the wind?

Alone
June 20, 2014

Looking around.
Emptiness surrounds.
Alone.
I don't hear a sound.
I feel bound.
Alone.

Calling
June 20, 2014

I hear my call.
I jump but fall.
I try to stall.
I hear them call.
I jump and fall.

Gone
June 20, 2014

I had a thought.
Now it's gone.
An idea lost.
Thoughts and ideas.
Just gone.

Night
June 20, 2014

Outside I prefer the moon.
Daybreak comes too soon.
The night is still.
The stars could kill.
The night is still.

Grief
June 21, 2014

I don't know what happened.
Today was fine.
And now grief.
Grief.

Grey Skies
June 22, 2014

Grey skies fade to black.
From some things you can't turn back.
I regret my last attack.
A hard punch I did pack.
Grey skies fade to black.
I. Am. Sorry.

Lost
June 22, 2014

I have found myself lost.
I guess that's the cost.
Of the decisions I made.
Into nothing I fade.
I am lost.

River
June 22, 2014

This river flows.
But where it goes.
No one knows.
This path I chose.
To follow the river flows.

Stitches
June 22, 2014

Sewing my heart back together.
Stitches.
I feel it breaking.
Pulling against the mend.
Stitches.
Will this ever stop?

Love
June 23, 2014

What is love?
Is it something sent from above?
Or is it something meant to confuse us?
Something just to start a fuss.
What is love?
Is it something sent from above?
Or is it something meant to cause chaos?
I don't know; I'm at a lose.

Lost Again
June 24, 2014

I feel lost.
I guess that's the cost.
For the actions I chose.
At least no one knows.
The decisions have been made.
The price is being paid.
I am lost.

Happiness
June 24, 2014

Happiness is a choice.
Let people hear your voice.
Happiness is up to you.
To be happy, do what you must do.
Happiness is bliss.
If you're looking for advice, take this.

Baby Deer
June 29, 2014

A weekend outdoor.
I couldn't ask for more.
The beauty here.
It is nothing to fear.
This morning I saw a baby deer.

Fourth of July
June 30, 2014

The Fourth of July.
Fireworks fly.
Our nation is free.
What more could there be?
To those who serve, our thanks we owe.
So we may have the Fourth we know.

www.ingramcontent.com/pod-product-compliance
Ingram Content Group UK Ltd.
Pitfield, Milton Keynes, MK11 3LW, UK
UKHW041904190726
13854UKWH00003B/1074

9 781312 320963